For Loraine & Mark

An Imprint of Sterling Publishing
387 Park Avenue South
New York, NY 10016

ISBN 978-1-4351-4730-0

Manufactured in China
Lot #:
2  4  6  8  10  9  7  5  3  1
03/13

# PING & PONG

## ARE BEST FRIENDS

### (mostly)

## Tim Hopgood

Sandy Creek
NEW YORK

Anything Ping can do,

Pong can do better.

**Anything?**
Yes, anything!

Ping likes ice-skating.

Pong does too!

Ping likes painting.

Pong does too!

Ping likes fishing.

Ping is learning to squeak French.

Pong can already squeak in nine different languages.

Ping decided enough was enough.

He was never going to be the **BEST** at **anything**.

So Ping sat down and did **NOTHING.**

"What are you doing?" asked Pong.
**"NOTHING,"** replied Ping.

"Oh!" said Pong.
"I've never tried doing
that before. What do
you have to do?"

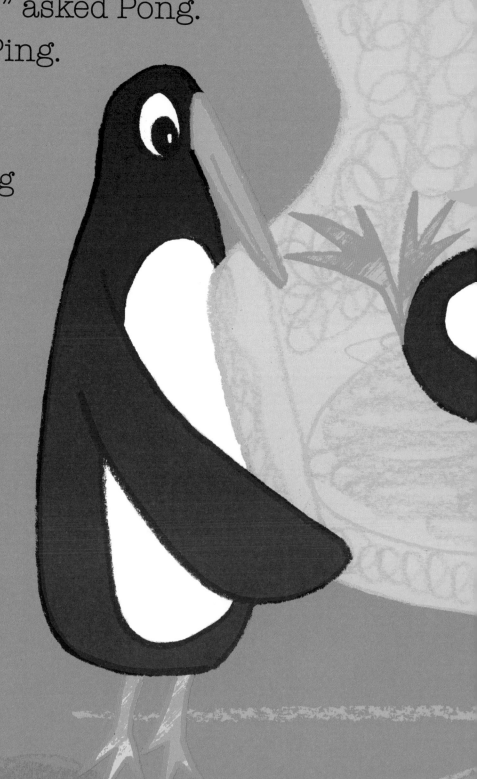

"**NOTHING,**" replied Ping.
"Oh, I see," said Pong.

And Pong went off to
practice doing **NOTHING**.

Pong tried as hard as he could,
but he just couldn't do it.

Doing nothing was **IMPOSSIBLE**.

How does Ping do it? he wondered.

Pong decided he didn't like doing nothing.

But doing other things without
Ping wasn't much fun.

So he wrote Ping a letter.

Dear Ping,
If you can spare the time,
I wondered if you would
like to come and play.
I miss you.

Pong x

Ping didn't open the letter straight away.

He was too busy . . .

. . . doing nothing.

Finally Ping read the letter.

He realized he missed his friend too.

The next day,
Ping made some cookies.

And then he went to visit Pong.

Even though they were a bit burnt,

Pong said they were the nicest cookies he'd ever tasted.

Pong had also done some baking.

TO THE BEST FRIEND IN THE WORLD

And, at last,
Ping realized he
**was** THE BEST
at something after all.